For Davy – best grandpa ever! V. F.   For Michele – who is essential. D. K.

First published 2004 by Walker Books Ltd, 87 Vauxhall Walk, London SE11 5HJ

2 4 6 8 10 9 7 5 3 1

Text © 2004 Vivian French   Illustrations © 2004 Dana Kubick

The right of Vivian French and Dana Kubick to be identified as author and illustrator respectively of this work
has been asserted by them in accordance with the Copyright, Designs and Patents Act 1988

This book has been typeset in Minion Condensed

Printed in Singapore

British Library Cataloguing in Publication Data: a catalogue record for this book is available from the British Library

ISBN 0-7445-8699-2

www.walkerbooks.co.uk

I Love You, Grandpa

Written by
Vivian French

Illustrated by
Dana Kubick

WALKER BOOKS
AND SUBSIDIARIES
LONDON • BOSTON • SYDNEY • AUCKLAND

Grandpa had come to stay for the weekend.
"I'm going to work," Mum said.
"Rex, Flora and Queenie – look after Stanley!"

"Who shall I look after?"
Stanley asked.
Mum laughed. "You can
look after Grandpa!"
And she waved goodbye.

Goodbye,
Mum.

"Right," said Grandpa, "what would you like to do?"

"We could go to the playground," Stanley said hopefully, "and swing on the swings!"
"I want to play football!" Rex said. "I'm good at football."

Rex kicked the ball
to Grandpa,

but Grandpa
missed it.

Stanley tried
to save it,

*I'll get it,
Grandpa!*

but
he fell over.

Oops

"H'mph," said Rex. "You're
not much good at
football, are you, Grandpa!"
And he went off to
practise by himself.

"Could you twirl my
rope for me, Grandpa?"
Queenie asked.

"I'll hold the other end,"
said Stanley.

I'll help!

The rope wriggled,
but it didn't twirl.
"Oh dear," said Grandpa.

"My end didn't work either,"
Stanley said sadly.

"I'll go and skip on my own," Queenie said, and she walked away.

"What about jumping?"
Flora suggested.

"How high can you jump,
Grandpa?"

Grandpa couldn't jump very high at all.

"Try again, Grandpa! You do it like this," said Stanley. Grandpa was too puffed to answer.

"Perhaps you're too old for jumping, Grandpa," Flora said, and she went to skip with Queenie.

"Are you tired, Grandpa?"
Stanley asked as
Grandpa sat down
with a loud sigh.
"Just a bit," said Grandpa.

"Poor Grandpa."
Stanley climbed up
beside him.
"I'll look after you. I'll
sing you a song. Mum
always sings me a song
when I'm tired."

Stanley sang Grandpa a song.

I love bees 'cos they go buzz buzz buzz

And I love little fishies when they go splishy sploshy splishy

And I love worms when they

wiggle wiggle wiggle

But most of all I love my Grandpa because he is lovely

and I love him best of all...

Grandpa listened,
and his eyes slowly closed.
Stanley snuggled up close,
and Grandpa snored
a little snore...
Stanley shut his eyes,
and they slept
peacefully ...

until Mum came home.

"Ooof!" said Grandpa, rubbing
  his eyes.
"Stanley!" said Mum. "Have you
  been tiring Grandpa out?"
"No!" said Stanley. "I've been
  looking after Grandpa!"
"He's looked after me
  so well," said Grandpa,
"I'm going to take
  him to the swings."

"We're coming too!" said Rex,
Flora and Queenie.
"Splendid!" said Grandpa.
"Are you ready,
Stanley?"

"Hurrah!" said Stanley.

"I love you, Grandpa!"